For all of the wonderful GLAM fans—this one's for you! —T. S.

Let your light shine in everything you do. —V. B.-N.

union square kids

NEW YORK

UNION SQUARE KIDS and the distinctive Union Square Kids logo are trademarks of Sterling Publishing Co., LLC.

Union Square & Co., LLC, is a subsidiary of Sterling Publishing Co., Inc.

Text © 2022 Tammi Sauer
Illustrations © 2022 Vanessa Brantley-Newton

ISBN 978-1-4549-3303-8

Library of Congress Control Number: 2022930489

For information about custom editions, special sales, and premium purchases,
please contact specialsales@unionsquareandco.com

Printed in China

Lot #:
2 4 6 8 10 9 7 5 3 1

04/22

unionsquareandco.com

Designed by Jo Obarowski

Mary Had a Little Plan

by Tammi Sauer

illustrated by
Vanessa Brantley-Newton

union
square
kids

NEW YORK

Mary had a little plan
that sprouted on the SPOT.

It all began the day she passed
a drab, abandoned lot.

A stretch of mess, a marked-up wall,
the ground was wild with weeds.

Then Mary took a look around.
"I know what this place needs."

"A **cleanup** and an **overhaul**.
A garden path or two . . .

The right design will be **divine**.
There's tons that I can do!"

So Mary wheeled in **cans** of paint and **trimmings** for the trees.

She studied every fabric choice.
The possibilities!

She sent requests to local shops
for **flowers**, **tools**, and **wood**,

and trucks soon barreled down the road
to help the neighborhood.

Then Mary gathered
bags of **trash**.
It took her half the day.

The sight of so much left to do consumed her with **dismay**.

"Oh, what a **mess**. I must **confess**, I'm really in a **bind**."

But when a spider sat beside her
something came to **mind**.

So Mary asked her friends for **help**.
They didn't **hesitate**.

"**Hooray!**" said Mary. "Follow me.
It's time to **renovate!**"

Soon Bo Peep's sheep went in knee-deep.
They **chomped** the weeds away.

A clean-up crew knew what to do to fix the **disarray**.

The flowerbeds were organized
in **neat** and **tidy** rows,

while Jack and Jill went up the hill
and watered with the **hose**.

Miss Muffet crafted **cozy seats**,
as others worked the wall.
Another built a **nook for books**,
and they were free for all.

With **twinkling lights** strung overhead
and grass beneath her feet,
sweet Mary added one more thing
to make the scene complete.

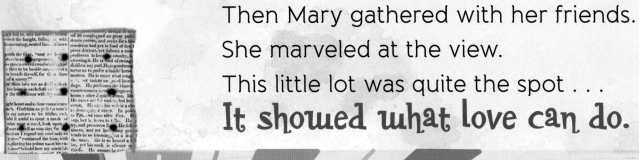

Then Mary gathered with her friends.
She marveled at the view.
This little lot was quite the spot . . .
It showed what love can do.